BL 2.8
Pts 0.5

Animal STORYBOOKS

The Proud Pelican's Secret

Story by Rebecca Johnson
Photos by Steve Parish

GARETH**STEVENS**
GS
P U B L I S H I N G
A Member of the WRC Media Family of Companies

Please visit our web site at: www.garethstevens.com
For a free color catalog describing Gareth Stevens Publishing's list of high-quality books
and multimedia programs, call 1-800-542-2595 (USA) or 1-800-387-3178 (Canada).
Gareth Stevens Publishing's fax: (414) 332-3567.

Library of Congress Cataloging-in-Publication Data

Johnson, Rebecca, 1966–
    [Pelican's pride]
    The proud pelican's secret / story by Rebecca Johnson; photos by Steve Parish. — North American ed.
        p. cm. — (Animal storybooks)
    Summary: Mr. Pelican, who is so very proud of his looks, guards a secret about his fantastic fishing ability.
    ISBN 0-8368-5974-X (lib. bdg.)
    [1. Pelicans—Fiction. 2. Pride and vanity—Fiction.] I. Parish, Steve, ill. II. Title.
    PZ7.J63637Pel 2005
    [E]—dc22   2005042877

First published as *Pelican's Pride* in 2002 by Steve Parish Publishing Pty Ltd, Australia.
Text copyright © 2002 by Rebecca Johnson. Photos copyright © 2002 by Steve Parish Publishing.
Series concept by Steve Parish Publishing.

This U.S. edition first published in 2006 by
Gareth Stevens Publishing
A Member of the WRC Media Family of Companies
330 West Olive Street, Suite 100
Milwaukee, Wisconsin 53212 USA

This edition copyright © 2006 by Gareth Stevens, Inc.

Gareth Stevens series editor: Dorothy L. Gibbs
Gareth Stevens cover and title page designs: Dave Kowalski

Printed in the United States of America

1 2 3 4 5 6 7 8 9 09 08 07 06 05

Mr. Pelican thought that he was the most handsome seabird in the whole world.

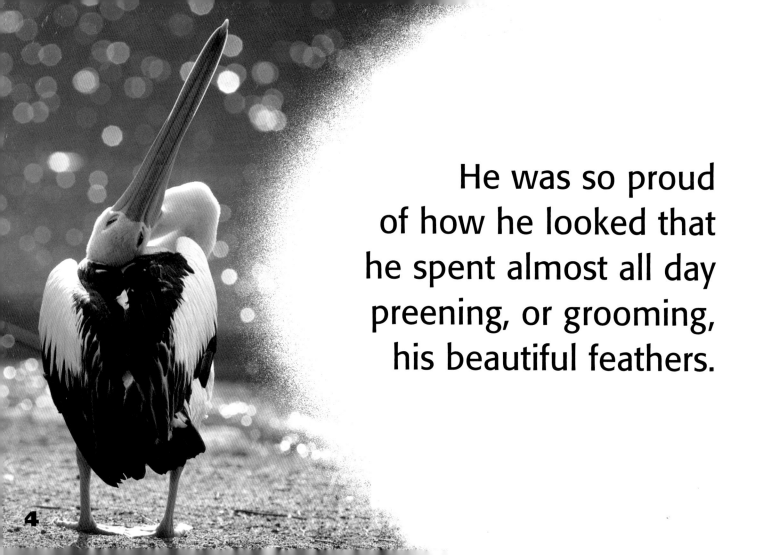

He was so proud
of how he looked that
he spent almost all day
preening, or grooming,
his beautiful feathers.

4

Then he spent
the rest of the day
looking at his reflection
in the water.

"How do you do it?"
the other pelicans would ask.

"How do you keep your tummy so full when you never spend time fishing?"

"Oh, I'm a fantastic fisherman!"
Mr. Pelican boasted.

But the other pelicans were still puzzled.
They spent most of each day on the water,
catching and eating fish.

First, they beat
their wings
to round up
schools of fish.
Then, they scooped
the fish into their bills.

Fishing
was hard work
and did not leave
much time for grooming.

"Mr. Pelican must have a trick," they decided.

"We should follow him to see how he gets his food so easily."

The next day,
when the pelicans
went fishing, one of them
stayed behind. He flew
up onto a power line
and sat there to keep
an eye on Mr. Pelican.

Thinking that all
of the other pelicans
had gone fishing,
sneaky Mr. Pelican
took off and flew
high in the sky.

Then, the pelican on the power line saw Mr. Pelican race along the beach and land near some fishing boats.

The men on the fishing boats spotted Mr. Pelican and threw leftover fish from their catch to him — which Mr. Pelican guzzled down greedily.

The next day, when Mr. Pelican arrived
at his favorite fishing spot, he was surprised
to find all the other pelicans there, too.

Now, they
all enjoy
the fishermen's
leftovers . . .

. . . and spend the rest of the day making their feathers look beautiful.